THE BOXCAR CHILDREN®

CREATED BY
GERTRUDE CHANDLER WARNER

BOOK

150

THE HUNDRED-YEAR MYSTERY

ILLUSTRATED BY
ANTHONY VanARSDALE

ALBERT WHITMAN & COMPANY
CHICAGO, ILLINOIS

Copyright © 2019 by Albert Whitman & Company
First published in the United States of America
in 2019 by Albert Whitman & Company

ISBN 978-0-8075-0748-3 (hardcover)
ISBN 978-0-8075-0749-0 (paperback)

Printed in the United States of America
10 9 8 7 6 5 4 3 2 1 LB 22 21 20 19 18

Illustrations by Anthony VanArsdale

Visit the Boxcar Children online at www.boxcarchildren.com.
For more information about Albert Whitman & Company,
visit our website at www.albertwhitman.com.

100 years of Albert Whitman & Company
Celebrate with us in 2019!

Contents

Will There Be Ghosts?

Ghosts, ghosts, ghosts. Will there be ghosts? Six-year-old Benny Alden biked far behind his brother and sisters. Usually he pedaled the fastest, leading the way. Not today. Not where they were going.

Benny could see the others far ahead. Fourteen-year-old Henry was in front. Twelve-year-old Jessie and ten-year-old Violet biked close behind. The curvy bike path led away from Greenfield. The Aldens had never followed this path before. They never had a reason to go this way. Until now.

Will there be ghosts? Benny shivered. He fell farther and farther behind. *Ghosts, ghosts, ghosts.* That's all he'd thought about since breakfast—since what Grandfather had said.

***

This morning at breakfast, Benny had talked and talked and talked about his hundred-day project. Everyone at Benny's school needed to collect one hundred of something, or make one hundred of something, or do one hundred somethings. But Benny couldn't think of one hundred of anything that wasn't boring.

He'd tried a bunch of things. Gluing one hundred pennies on ping-pong paddles? *Bor-ing*. Stringing one hundred pieces of popcorn? *Bor-ing*. Bending one hundred pipe cleaners into animal shapes? *Bor-ing*. His best idea had been to collect one hundred worms. For two days he dug all around the backyard. But he only found ten worms. He set them free.

Then, at breakfast, Grandfather had asked, "How would the four of you like to take a tour of Wintham Manor?"

"Isn't that the giant gray house on the hill?" Jessie asked.

"That's Wintham Manor, all right," said Grandfather. "No one's lived there for a hundred years."

Will There Be Ghosts?

"Why not?" Benny asked.

Grandfather wiggled his eyebrows and said, "That is one of the many mysteries of Wintham Manor. My friend Ella leads tours there and said you're welcome to come. She told me the Manor will be one hundred years old next month." Grandfather smiled at Benny. "With all your talk of one hundred this and one hundred that, I think a hundred-year-old house is a perfect place to visit."

"But," Benny said, "I can't carry a whole house to school for my project."

Grandfather had laughed. "No, I expect not. But Wintham Manor might give you a helpful idea or two. Besides, the four of you have been wanting to bike to someplace you've never been before. Today seems a perfect day for a new adventure."

***

Henry, Jessie, and Violet had all liked Grandfather's suggestion. So now the children were biking to visit the mysterious old house. What bothered Benny was why no one had lived in Wintham Manor for a hundred years. He could think of only one good reason. *Ghosts.* People were afraid to live in

Wintham Manor...because it was haunted!

In the distance, Henry and the girls biked up a hill past a group of tall rocks. Benny shuddered. The rocks looked like giant fingers reaching up out of the ground. A few minutes later he got to the rocks and stopped. They didn't look as scary close up. Benny noticed something strange on the tallest finger. Someone had carved marks near the bottom. The markings were old and worn. They sort of looked like words, but different.

What if it's a warning? Benny wondered. What if it means "danger"? Benny jumped on his bike, pedaling as fast as he could until he caught up with the others.

As the sun moved higher in the sky, the bike path took a sharp curve along a creek. That's when the children saw the manor. The dirty stone building stood like a castle on the next hill. Henry stuck his right arm out and down. It was their signal to stop. The Aldens stared at the giant house. A dark cloud passed over it. Benny's heart thumped as the house fell into the shadow of the cloud.

One corner of Wintham Manor was a huge stone

tower. Violet pointed to the top. "Look at that big window," she said. "It's like the tower where Rapunzel let down her hair."

"The whole house looks like something out of a fairy tale," said Jessie.

"Or a scary movie," said Benny, "with ghosts."

"Wintham Manor is not scary," said Jessie. "It's just old."

"How do you know?" Benny asked.

"Because," said Jessie, "Grandfather would never send us anyplace like that."

Henry smiled. "I wouldn't let anything hurt my favorite little brother. Not even some old ghost."

Jessie knew how to move Benny's mind away from ghosts. "I could use some water and a snack before we bike up that hill," she said.

"Me too!" said Benny, opening his backpack. He still wasn't sure about ghosts, but he was sure he was hungry. Benny unwrapped a fig bar and started talking about his hundred-day project...again.

Jessie sighed. "Benny, you're really going to have to choose a project soon." She tore open a small bag of pretzels. "Maybe it won't be perfect, but it has to be *something*."

Benny stuck out his jaw. "It's not my fault I was sick when the hundred-day project started," he said. "By the time I got back to school, all the good ideas were taken." Benny folded the entire cookie into his mouth.

"I tried to give you one hundred buttons," said Jessie, "and Violet offered a hundred colored pencils, and Henry said you could pick out a hundred nails."

"Mgshwidlfhst." Benny tried to speak, but his mouth was too full.

Henry laughed. "What did you say?"

"Benny," whispered Violet, "you should finish chewing before you talk."

Benny chewed and chewed. Then he swallowed. "I want my project to be something really, *really* different," he said finally.

The children ate their snacks in silence. This was going to be one project Benny would have to figure out for himself. When they finished, Jessie collected their garbage into a bag to throw away later. She looked around at the blue creek and the green trees and the big manor on the next hill. It gave her an idea. "If we have time," she said, "I'd like Violet to take a few photos for my blog."

Jessie's blog was called *Where in Greenfield?* Every week she posted a photo of something around town—a tree house, a playground, a statue. Her readers sent in guesses about where in Greenfield the photo was taken. The next week, Jessie blogged the answer and posted a new photo. She thought the creek would be the perfect place for this week's entry.

Henry checked his watch and said, "Okay, let's meet back here in fifteen minutes."

Violet pulled her camera from her bike basket. Jessie took out the notebook and pen she always carried in her pocket. As the girls went exploring, the boys took off their shoes and socks and waded into the creek. A swarm of tadpoles darted away. "I could bring one hundred tadpoles for my project," said Benny.

Henry laughed. "You would have to catch them first." He picked up a flat stone and skipped it across the water. The stone skipped five times. He found another stone for Benny. "Hold it sideways, like this," said Henry. He moved Benny's fingers around the edges. Benny's first stone sank. But after a few tries, Benny could skip a stone two and three times.

For a while, Benny forgot about the project. But when they stopped skipping stones, the thoughts came back. "I'll never have a good idea," he said. "Never, ever, *ever*."

"Sometimes," said Henry, "when I have a problem I can't solve, I just stop thinking about it."

"Huh?" said Benny.

"I know it sounds strange," Henry said. "But when I ignore my problem, I get busy doing other things."

"Like what?" asked Benny.

"Like building that new doghouse for Watch or fixing Grandfather's record player or going for a long run. Pretty soon the answer to my problem sneaks up on me. The more I ignore it, the closer it comes. Then, one day, the answer jumps in front of me and shouts, 'Here I am!'"

Benny thought about this. "So, I should stop worrying about the project?" he asked.

"That's right," said Henry. "Let's go to Wintham Manor to see what a hundred-year-old house looks like. I bet watching out for ghosts makes you forget all about your problem."

Henry lay back on the bank of the creek and closed his eyes. Benny lay back and watched puffy clouds change into different shapes: a dog, a bear, a shoe, a snowman. He liked listening to the sound of water in the creek. He liked feeling the cool ground under him. This place reminded him of when the children lived in the woods.

After their parents died, the Alden children had run away from home. They had been afraid to go and live with their grandfather because they thought he would be mean. The children searched and searched for a place to live. Then one night, they took shelter in an old railroad car in the woods. They decided to make that boxcar their home. They even found a dog named Watch and kept him as their pet. The children had many adventures in the boxcar. They even played in a creek just like this one. Then they met Grandfather, who had been searching for them. He wasn't mean at all! Now the children lived with Grandfather in Greenfield. They used the boxcar as their clubhouse.

Just as Benny was starting to relax, Violet and Jessie came back.

"Time to hit the road," said Henry.

This time Benny kept up with the others. He still wasn't sure he wanted to meet ghosts. But, together, he knew the four of them could face whatever was waiting for them at Wintham Manor.

Curiouser and Curiouser

The Aldens climbed the stone steps and stared at the manor door.

"This is strange," said Henry. The doorway was so low that anyone taller than him would have to bend to enter. Henry gripped the heavy door knocker and banged it once. The sound echoed through the old house.

"Nobody's home," said Benny. "Let's go."

"Hang on," said Henry. "Grandfather's friend is supposed to be here." Henry knocked again. Still no answer. He knocked a third time.

"Coming, COME-ing," called a singsong voice. "Hold your horses. Hooooold your horses."

A key rattled in the giant lock. Slowly, the door

creaked open. But no one was there.

"Ghost!" cried Benny.

"Where?" A smiling face peeked around the door. "Oh. You mean me?"

A small woman stepped out. She was barely as tall as Violet. Silky black hair flowed down her back. She wore a long, old-fashioned dress. A pair of bright purple sneakers peeked out from under her skirt. "You must be James's grandchildren. I've been expecting you. I'm Ella Nakamol. Come in, come in. Welcome to Wintham Manor."

The children stepped into a large hall. Violet gasped. "That's beautiful." A giant mural of Greenfield covered one of the walls. It showed the town before there were wide streets or tall buildings.

Ella grunted as she pushed the door closed behind them. "I think this is the heaviest door in the world," she said.

"Why is the doorway so low?" asked Violet.

"Low?" Ella said. "Why, it seems just right to me. Now, how can I help you? James mentioned something about a hundred something-something."

"A hundred-day project," said Benny.

"What's that?" asked Ella.

"It's for school," Benny said. "I have to bring in a hundred of something or make a hundred of something. It's so I can learn what a hundred looks like."

"Why," said Ella, "one hundred looks exactly like *this*. Everything in this house is at least a hundred years old...except me, of course."

Ella laughed as she led the children through another low doorway into a grand living room. Violet followed slowly. This was such a beautiful old house—polished wood floors, beautiful rugs, carved furniture—everything delighted her artist's eye. Although, it did seem strange that all the doorways were built so low.

"We're usually closed today," said Ella. "Wintham Manor is an historic home people can visit. Like George Washington's home in Mount Vernon, Virginia, or Abraham Lincoln's in Springfield, Illinois. But, seeing as how you're my dear friend James's grandchildren, I'm planning to give you my Super-Duper Deeee-luxe Tour." She whispered, "Not many have seen what I'm going to show you today."

Benny stepped back. "Are there ghosts?" he asked.

Ella sighed. "I keep hoping," she said. "But so far I haven't met a one."

***

Bor-ing, Benny thought as he wandered around the living room. Jessie and Violet oohed and aahed over plumpy sofas and lumpy chairs. Violet took pictures for Jessie's *Where in Greenfield?* blog.

"We've kept the manor exactly the way Mr. Wintham left it one hundred years ago," Ella said. "People used to rent this first floor for parties—birthdays, weddings, holidays, and such." She fluffed a pillow. A cloud of dust poofed up. "But lately, it seems folks prefer the newer, fancier party places in town."

"Wow, check this out," called Henry from under an old table. Benny crawled under to look. "They don't build tables like this anymore," said Henry, excited. "See these nails? Each one is a little different because they were all made by hand."

The nails looked like ordinary nails to Benny. He climbed back out. *Bor-ing.*

There wasn't one single fun thing here for

Benny's hundred-day project. After a while, he almost hoped for a ghost—or one hundred of them. Benny walked through another small doorway that led to a big stairway. *Wow!* Paintings and drawings and photos covered the huge wall all the way up the stairs. There were wacky cartoon characters, planets with square moons, bicycles with twenty wheels.

Benny climbed the stairs slowly, looking at every single thing. Even the old photos were fun to look at. Women wore old-fashioned dresses like Ella's. Boys wore short pants with suspenders. Benny stopped in front of a large photo of a tall man. The man was planting a baby tree. Benny looked closer. The man had the biggest mustache Benny had ever seen.

"Bingo!" cried Ella. Benny jumped. He hadn't heard the others come up the stairs. Ella pointed at the photo of the man with the mustache. "You're looking at the one, the only Mr. Alfred Wintham," she said. "This is the only photo we have of him. We think it was taken a hundred years ago, just before he...before he..." Ella sniffed. "Poor Mr. Wintham barely got the chance to live here. He'd

just finished building the manor and planting some trees and hanging up his artwork when a terrible flu epidemic swept through town."

"What's an epi...epi..." Benny couldn't remember the word.

"Epidemic," said Ella. "It's when many, many people become sick at the same time with the same illness."

"Mr. Wintham died?" whispered Violet. Ella nodded. Violet looked at the wall of paintings and drawings. "And he was the artist of all these?"

"He had quite the imagination," said Ella. "Come on, there are more surprises upstairs."

Whirrrr. Bzzzzzz. Whirrr. A noise made the children stop on the landing. It was coming from outside. They looked out the window into the backyard. A big man with a chain saw stood on a tall ladder. He was cutting limbs off an old tree. A yellow truck in the driveway had the words *Levi's Lumber—Cut and Carried* on the door. The man sawed off the last branch and climbed down the ladder. Then he began sawing the trunk. *Whirrrr. Bzzzzzz.*

"That's the tree Mr. Wintham planted the day he moved in," said Ella. "Sadly, it's sick and must be cut down."

Suddenly, the tree cutter yelled, "Timbeeeerrrrrr!"

The Aldens held their breaths as the tree tilted slowly, slowly, slowly away from the house. *KABOOM!* It crashed to the ground in an explosion of bark and twigs and leaves.

The tree cutter happened to look up at the window and see the Aldens. Ella opened the window. "Hi, Levi, there's a big plate of warm snickerdoodles in the kitchen and cold milk in the fridge."

The man smiled and waved.

"That's my brother, Levi," said Ella. "He helps keep the manor shipshape. Now, I'm going to show you the second floor. Only VIPs—Very Important People—have ever seen what you're about to see."

The children followed her up the wide staircase and around a corner, to...a brick wall.

"Where do we go now?" asked Jessie.

"Benny," said Ella, "would you grab that chipped bottom brick and give it a tug?"

Benny found the brick and pulled. He jumped

back as the wall slid open.

"A secret passageway!" said Henry.

Ella laughed. "Oh, this is just the beginning."

The children entered a long hallway. More of Alfred Wintham's artwork covered the walls. Mobiles hung from the ceiling. "But...but where are the rooms?" asked Violet.

"Oh, dear, did I lose those rooms again?" asked Ella. "No, wait, I do believe they're here." She pointed to a painting of a clown with a large red nose. "Henry, would you be so kind as to push the clown's nose?"

Henry pushed, and another hidden door swung open. The children followed Ella into a large room. Funny, bright-colored creatures were painted on the walls. There were blue, red, green, and yellow tables and chairs of all sizes. "It looks like study hall at school," said Jessie, "except way more fun."

The children returned to the main hallway. Every room had a secret way of opening its door—a floorboard you jumped on, a lever you pulled. One room had a staircase that led nowhere. Another had shelves filled with colorful blocks and wood puzzles. In the Art Room, Violet sat at a big drawing table. She imagined all the wonderful art she could create using the boxes of colorful pencils, old ink pens, bits of charcoal, and tubes of paint.

When the children finished exploring all of the rooms, they gathered in the hallway. "I've never seen a house built like this," Henry told Ella. "Hidden rooms, secret passageways, fun ways to open doors. Who designed this?"

"Alfred Wintham designed every nook and cranny," Ella said.

Jessie looked around. "I agree it's fun to visit," she said. "But I'm not sure grown-ups would like living here. They'd have to duck through doorways and push clown's noses and pull chipped bricks."

"Maybe that's why no one bought the house after Mr. Wintham died," said Ella. "We're lucky Greenfield bought the manor so everyone could come visit."

Benny reached up to the painting of the clown and pushed the clown's nose. He laughed as the door closed. "Why did Mr. Wintham build the house this way?" he asked.

"That is a wonderful question," said Ella. "But

whatever plans Alfred Wintham had for this house died with him. It seems he never told anyone and never left a message of any kind. This manor is really a mystery. A hundred-year-old mystery that I don't think we'll ever solve."

"Well," said Henry, "thanks for showing us around. It's been great."

"Oh," said Ella. She paused. "So I guess you don't want to see..."

"See what?" asked Benny.

Ella looked around, then whispered, "The secret, secret, *secret* place."

"I do. I do," said Benny.

Ella led them through a door at the end of the hall and up a twisty staircase to the top floor. Everything was child sized—the doorways, the rooms, the hidden passages. They followed Ella up, down, and all around.

"It's like a maze," said Jessie.

One passageway opened into the stone tower. "Look," said Violet, pointing up, "there's Rapunzel's window." Sunshine poured through the window near the top of the tower.

But the tower looked wrong to Violet. "The inside of this tower seems too narrow," she said. "The tower looks much bigger from the outside."

"I've noticed that too," said Ella. "I've always thought they built it with bricks between the inside and the outside walls. That would make the tower stronger. We wouldn't want those heavy stones falling down."

High up, a platform ran all the way around the tower. It reminded Henry of his school's running track that circled above the gym floor. "Can we go up there?" he asked.

"I'm afraid not," Ella said. "There used to be a rope ladder hanging from that beam." She pointed to a thick wood beam that ran across the center of the tower. A scrap of rope still hung from the middle. "That ladder was gone years before I came to work here. I was told the view from the platform is amazing. You can see out that window for miles. But I guess the rope became old and unsafe, so they took it down. I've always wondered if some secrets might be tucked away up there."

Greenfield's town bell clanged in the distance.

Henry checked his watch. "We'd better go," he said. "We have a long ride home."

"Let me pack you up some snickerdoodles for the road," said Ella. "I'll meet you outside."

Out front, Violet said, "Let me take a picture of all of you next to the manor."

Henry, Jessie, and Benny quickly stood next to a big white stone at the corner of the house. As Violet focused her camera, the Levi's Lumber truck rattled down the driveway.

"Let me help you," called Levi, climbing out. "I'll take the photo so you can all be in it."

Violet handed him the camera and joined the others. "Move a little to the right," Levi told Henry. "You'll want that cornerstone in the photo." Levi took several pictures and returned the camera to Violet. "If you want to photograph something really interesting," he said, "I'll be back in a couple days to cut that hundred-year-old tree trunk into slices." He climbed back into his truck and waved as the truck rattled away.

Jessie traced her fingers along the letters chiseled into the white cornerstone. It said *Alfred*

Wintham Manor and was followed by the year, one hundred years ago.

Benny noticed a chip in the stone that looked like the chip in the brick upstairs. He gripped the stone and pulled. A chunk of the cornerstone fell away.

"Oh no," he said, quickly picking up the stone. He tried to put it back. "It won't go."

"Let me," said Henry. He took the chunk of stone and was about to put it back. "Hey," he said, "it's hollow inside." He reached his hand into the cornerstone. "There's something in here!"

Cold Clues and Warm Cookies

Henry pulled out a large cylinder with gray metal caps on both ends. "What is it?" asked Benny.

"It looks like the capsule we use at the bank drive-through," said Violet.

The children loved folding the money they saved into the capsule. Then they slid the capsule into a tube. *Whoosh!* Air sucked the capsule through the tube right from their car all the way into the bank.

"Those capsules are airtight," said Henry. "I wonder if this one is." Gripping one end, he gave it a hard twist. *Pfffffssssstttt.* Air hissed out. Startled, Henry dropped the capsule. It clanked to the ground. A small book slid out.

Benny reached for it. "Wait," said Jessie. "Be

really, really careful. It might be fragile."

"You do it," said Benny.

Very gently, Jessie picked up the book and smoothed it with her hand. "The pages are still nice and soft," she said. "The capsule protected them from drying out in the air."

The words *A Journal for the Curious* were hand printed on the cover.

"*I'm* curious," said Benny.

Jessie opened the journal. The writing looked old-fashioned and fancy. She read:

> *In these pages you will find*
> *Clues to spark your curious mind*
> *Travel to my world long past*
> *To find my treasure trove at last*

"Treasure!" cried Benny. "But what's a 'trove'?"

"A 'treasure trove' just means a hidden treasure," explained Jessie.

"And the poem talks about traveling to a world in the past," said Violet. She loved reading books about people time-traveling to the past or the future.

Henry grinned. "I don't think this riddle means we'll really travel back in time," he said. "But it does say it has clues to finding treasure."

Jessie turned the pages. "What if this journal is like a treasure map?" she said. "Maybe, if we follow the clues, we'll find the—"

"Snickerdoodles!" called Ella. She carried a paper bag down the front steps. "Who wants some fresh-baked snickerdoodles?"

Benny rushed over. "We found a hidden treasure!" he said, grabbing Ella's hand. "Come look."

Ella hurried over. She froze when she saw the cornerstone. "Wha...what happened?"

"I just pulled," said Benny, "and it opened!"

Ella blinked. Then blinked again. "Oh my," she said softly. "Oh my. Oh my. Oh my." She sat on the ground, and the children gathered around her.

Jessie handed her the journal. "We found a time capsule with this inside."

Ella's hand shook as she took it. "Well...well...I mean...I never..." She opened the book and read the poem. "Whatever can this mean?"

"Do you know who put it in there?" asked Henry.

"I didn't even know there was a journal...or a secret hiding place. I just thought the cornerstone was an ordinary piece of stone telling when the manor was built." She tried to think. "I guess the stonemason who carved the cornerstone could have put it in. Or a construction worker. We really know so little about the history of the manor."

"I hope we haven't damaged anything," said Jessie.

Ella shook her head and brushed back her silky hair. "Actually, this could be quite wonderful, quite wonderful indeed." Suddenly, the smell of cinnamon filled the air. "Oh, gracious, I forgot your cookies." She passed around the bag of cookies. Bites of cinnamony, sugary snickerdoodles melted in the children's mouths.

"Ella," said Jessie, "you just said that this journal could be 'wonderful.' What did you mean?"

"Remember I told you that not many people come to Wintham Manor anymore?" Ella asked. "Well, the town has always helped pay to keep the manor going. But now the mayor said the town is thinking of tearing it down and building something new."

The Hundred-Year Mystery

"They can't tear it down!" said Violet. She loved this old house with its Rapunzel tower and hidden passages.

Ella held up the small journal. "I'm thinking this just might be the way to bring visitors back. Don't you think that folks would come to see a hidden cornerstone? And a time capsule? And a hundred-year-old journal with a mystery inside?"

"And there's a treasure!" said Benny. "The poem says there are clues."

"Let's see." Ella turned to the next page. "Ah, here we go." She read:

> *Come find my home away from home*
> *From which I traveled to worlds unknown*
> *Where I was raised from all my brothers*
> *Known to me, but not the others*
>
> *Go to where the sun's first ray*
> *Shines just east of town each day*
> *Then plumb a line both straight and true*
> *And dig there for your second clue*

"What does that mean?" asked Benny.

No one had an answer.

Ella hugged the small journal. She closed her eyes and swayed slowly side to side. Violet could tell how much this all meant to Ella. She reached over and gently patted Ella's shoulder.

Ella looked at Violet and smiled. "Here," she said, handing Violet the journal. "James has told me how much his grandchildren love mysteries. He said you've helped solve quite a few. I'm too old to be running around town trying to figure out riddles. Besides, I need to stay here to run the manor. Perhaps you can find the treasure. And maybe that treasure will be so wonderful it will save the manor."

Henry looked at his brother and sisters. They all nodded. He turned to Ella. "We'll try," he promised. "We'll do our best."

The path back to Greenfield was mostly downhill. It was an easy ride for four tired children. This time, Benny kept up. They hadn't met any ghosts at Wintham Manor. And Benny hadn't found anything for his hundred-day project. But they did find a word-map that might lead to a treasure. Solving this mystery was going to take some hard work. But, as Grandfather often said, "Nothing worth having comes easy."

CHAPTER 4

A Dangerous Climb

The smell of pancakes drifted out from the kitchen. It floated upstairs into each child's bedroom. One by one, they woke and shuffled downstairs. Watch sat next to the stove. His tail wagged as Grandfather cooked on a large griddle.

"Morning, sleepyheads," said Grandfather. "Breakfast's almost ready."

Jessie set out the plates. Benny folded napkins. Violet put out forks and knives. And Henry put out glasses and a pitcher of milk.

The night before, the children had told Grandfather about their adventure at the manor. They showed him the journal, and he had examined the fancy writing with his large magnifying glass.

He read and reread the riddle. But he couldn't figure it out either. "Let's all go to sleep thinking about it," he had said. "Our brains are amazing computers. Sometimes they do their best work while we sleep." But it hadn't helped. The riddle was just as confusing in the morning as it had been the night before.

Benny hopped up on a stool to watch Grandfather flipping pancakes. "Your pancakes smell different than Mrs. McGregor's," said Benny.

"Do they?" Grandfather asked. He leaned over and sniffed. "You're right," he said. "That's because Mrs. McGregor makes everything from scratch."

Mrs. McGregor was the Alden's housekeeper. She was on vacation in Ireland.

Grandfather slid a spatula under the pancakes. He began lifting them from the griddle onto a platter. "Since I'm not much of a cook, I made these pancakes with Panquake mix."

Benny laughed. "You mean pan*cake* mix."

"Nope," said Grandfather. He nodded at a box on the counter. Its big letters said *Panquakes—The pancake mix that's fun to fix.*

Jessie showed Benny the lettering. "See? The *name* of this pancake mix is Panquakes, so the first letter is a capital *P*."

Violet grinned. "Like the capital *V* in my name. The color violet doesn't have a capital *V*, but a person named Violet does."

"Well, however you spell it," said Benny, "I'm going to eat it."

Just as Grandfather finished putting the pancakes onto the platter, his office phone rang. "I've been expecting an important business call," he said, hurrying down the hall. "Go ahead and eat. I'll join you as soon as I can."

As Jessie lifted the platter of pancakes, a cool morning breeze blew through the kitchen window. "Let's picnic out at the boxcar," she said.

The children carried everything to a small table in the backyard. The table was made from an old board Henry had found in an alley. He had sanded the edges smooth, then gave the wood a coat of red paint. Finally, he set the board on cinder blocks next to the boxcar. Usually the table was big enough for their picnics, but this morning there wasn't enough room for everything. Henry had to set the pitcher of milk on the grass. "I should make a bigger table," said Henry. Still, they managed to enjoy the delicious breakfast. And, every now and then, a small bit of pancake just happened to fall off the table and into Watch's mouth.

Rays of sunshine shone through tree leaves. They made dancing patterns on the boxcar. "When we lived in the boxcar," said Violet, "I loved when the morning sun peeked through the door and woke me up."

"That's like the clue in the journal," Jessie said. "I memorized it as I went to sleep." Jessie liked to memorize all sorts of things: poems, bits of plays, songs. "Part of the clue said, 'Go to where the sun's first ray shines just east of town each day.'"

"But what town does it mean?" Henry asked. "How can we find the 'sun's first ray' if we don't know where the journal writer lived?"

The children ate their pancakes, trying to think of an answer to Henry's question. Violet drank her milk, which left a small, white mustache. Dabbing her lip with a napkin, she said, "Ella said the journal might have been written by someone who helped build the manor. If that person worked in Greenfield, maybe they lived here too."

"'The sun's first ray,'" said Henry. "Well, when the sun rises, the first thing it touches is high up, like the treetops. What high point is to the east of Greenfield?" Henry stabbed another pancake onto his plate and poured syrup over it.

"What about Rapunzel's tower?" said Jessie. "Maybe that's the highest point."

Henry finished his pancake and washed it down with milk. "What bothers me," he said, "is that the clue says the place is 'just east' of town. We had to bike east and then turn north to get to Wintham Manor."

Benny thought back to riding their bikes to the manor. He remembered pedaling up and up and up. "Rocks!" he said. "Those scary ones that look like fingers sticking out of the ground."

Henry jumped up. "That's it!" he said, excited. "Jessie, how does the rest of the poem go?"

A Dangerous Climb

Jessie closed her eyes and recited:

> *Come find my home away from home*
> *From which I traveled to worlds unknown*
> *Where I was raised from all my brothers*
> *Known to me, but not the others*

"I've got an idea," said Henry, heading for the garage. "I need to pack a couple of things. I'll meet you at our bikes when you finish eating. And, Jessie, bring the journal."

***

The children were out of breath by the time they reached the rocks. Henry slowed his bike at the tallest one. "The top of that rock is the highest point around," he said. "I'm going to climb up to see what I can see."

"Me too," said Benny.

"Not this time," said Henry. "It's too dangerous."

"But I can climb trees," said Benny.

Henry knelt down and rested his hands on Benny's shoulders. "You know I took a rock climbing course at camp. There are many special things you must learn to climb rocks safely. I don't want you getting hurt." Henry opened his backpack. He took out the small folding shovel they used for camping and handed it to Benny. "Wait for me right here," he said. "I'll have a very important job for you as soon as I reach the top."

Henry began climbing the finger rocks. The lower rocks were as easy to climb as the oak tree in their backyard. But the higher Henry climbed, the steeper the rocks became. There were fewer places to grip with his fingers and not as many ledges to push with his toes. His heart pounded from the hard climb. A few times he had to rest before climbing again.

"Please be careful," called Jessie.

Violet pressed her hands to her mouth, almost afraid to watch.

Benny hardly breathed. He knew Henry was strong. Still, this rock seemed as high as the sky.

Slowly, carefully, Henry climbed. Jessie watched him go higher and higher. "Oh my gosh," she said. "I just realized something." She ran to her bike and took out the journal. "Sometimes the same words

can mean two different things." She flipped to the page and read the clue.

> *Come find my home away from home*
> *From which I traveled to worlds unknown*
> *Where I was raised from all my brothers*
> *Known to me, but not the others*

Above them, Henry was nearly at the top. "I thought 'raised from all my brothers' meant 'brought up,'" said Jessie. "The way we're all being *raised* by Grandfather. But it can also mean 'raised' like 'be higher up' than all my brothers. The way Henry raised himself higher than us."

At last Henry reached the top of the tallest "finger." He pulled himself up onto the top. "Made it!" he called. The others cheered. The top of the rock was nice and flat. Henry sat and drank some water as he looked out. "Oh wow," he called. "I can see the whole town from up here. I think I can even see Elmford." After a minute, he took a ball of string and a horseshoe out of his backpack. He knotted one end of the string around the middle of the horseshoe. "What does the poem say about plumbing a line?" he called.

Jessie called up, "Then plumb a line both straight and true and dig there for your second clue."

Henry started looking around. "What's he doing?" asked Benny.

"Looking for a place to plumb a line," said Jessie.

"I don't know what that means," Benny said. "Is he looking for a plum to eat?"

"Ah," said Jessie. "I see why it's hard to understand." She reached into her back pocket and pulled out her small notebook. She flipped to the back where she kept a list titled Benny's New Words. She wrote: *Plum = fruit you eat. Plumb line = a straight line up and down.* "Henry wants to make a plumb line—a line straight down—from where he is to where we are. Look. I think he's found it."

Henry had found the only place on top of the rock where he could look straight down to where Benny was standing. Carefully, he lay down on his stomach. Inch by inch, he pulled himself forward until his head and arms hung over the edge. "Okay, Benny," he called, "get your shovel ready. I'm going to plumb a line down to you." Unwinding the ball of string, Henry lowered the horseshoe down and down and down. The weight of the horseshoe kept the string straight. Soon the ball of string had grown very small. The horseshoe dangled just above the ground. "Is the string plumb?" called Henry.

Benny looked up and down the string. It was tight and straight. "Yes," said Benny.

"Then dig right under the horseshoe for our second clue," said Henry.

Benny started digging. Jessie thought that she or Violet could have dug faster. But it was important to all of them to work as a team. Jessie had memorized the poem. Violet had suggested the author of the journal lived in Greenfield. Henry had climbed to where the "sun's first ray" shone on Greenfield. And now it was Benny's turn. Even though he was the smallest, he always did his part. Benny dug and dug. The hard dirt made for hard work. Just as he was beginning to think there was nothing there—*clank*—the shovel struck metal.

CHAPTER

The Only

"I found something!" yelled Benny.

Jessie and Violet crowded around.

"What is it?" asked Violet.

"I don't see anything," Jessie said.

Benny kept digging. A bit of metal began to show. Then a little more. Blisters stung his hands. Still Benny dug. Jessie could see his hands really hurt. "May I help?" she asked. Benny handed her the shovel. Jessie dug awhile then passed the shovel to Violet. More and more metal showed. Soon, Henry climbed down from the rock and finished digging. He lifted out a metal box.

"I'll open it," said Benny. But as hard as he tried, he could not pull off the lid.

"Let me look," said Henry. He ran his fingers around the edges. "It's sealed with wax. Probably to keep air from getting inside." Henry took a small screwdriver from his bike's tool kit and scraped off the hundred-year-old wax. He handed the box to Benny. "Now try it."

This time the top opened easily. Benny lifted out a thick book. *The Only* was printed in gold on a black cover. "What kind of clue is this?" asked Benny, passing it to Jessie.

"This book is very famous," Jessie said. "It was written in England over a hundred and fifty years ago."

"I'll bet the person who wrote the journal took this book up to the top of that rock," said Henry. "It's peaceful up there. A great place to read. What did the writer call it? 'My home away from home, from which I traveled to worlds unknown'?"

Violet took the book and ran her fingers lightly over the gold letters. "When I read books," she said, "I travel to new and different worlds in my mind. That must be what the clue means. But I wonder why the person buried *this* book."

The Only

"Well," said Jessie, "*The Only* is about an orphan—"

"Like us?" asked Benny.

"Not quite," said Jessie. "This orphan is an 'only.' That means they have no brothers or sisters."

"Do you think," Henry asked, "that the person who wrote the journal left *The Only* so we would know they're an orphan?"

"Yes," said Jessie. "An orphan who came here to read."

Violet looked puzzled. "But the clue says, 'Where I was raised from all my *brothers*.'"

This stumped everyone for a while. Then Jessie said, "The boy in *The Only* grew up in an orphanage. Maybe his 'brothers' were the other orphans."

"I never heard of an orphanage in Greenfield," said Henry. "Jessie, what does the next clue say?"

Jessie flipped through the journal and read:

> *The Only's life was my life too*
> *Hard work, no toys, joys but a few*
> *I grew up as this tale is told*
> *Although my town is not as old*

"You were right," said Violet. "They did grow up in an orphanage. Just like the character in the book. What else does it say?"

Jessie read:

> *I hope that this next clue still waits*
> *Inside my neighbor's friendly gates*
> *I asked that Tyler please pass down, my*
> *Brownie treats that caught our town*

Benny laughed. "That's funny. A brownie is a treat you eat. How can it catch anything?"

"I read a picture book about an elf called a brownie who helped with the housework when the family was asleep," said Violet.

"Or maybe it's a Brownie," Jessie said, "like I was before Girl Scouts. Brownie treats could be cookies."

"It could be a recipe for brownies," said Henry. He folded the shovel and put it back in his pack. "Whatever it is, I think we have to find the orphanage first. Once we do that, we can find the 'neighbor's friendly gates.' That's where we'll find the next clue."

The Only

Jessie put *The Only* back into the metal box. She set it carefully into her bike basket. "Let's check the library. They have a lot of information about Greenfield's history."

The children biked toward town. As they went, the yellow Levi's Lumber truck rumbled by on its way up to Wintham Manor. Levi honked and waved, then slowed the truck. "Remember to come take photos at the manor in the next few days," he called. "I'll be slicing up that big old tree. It's a pretty exciting thing to see."

"Hey," said Benny, "that rhymed."

Levi laughed. "By gosh, I'm a poet and didn't even know it!" And his hearty laugh trailed away as he drove off.

***

The children found librarian Trudy Silverton teetering at the top of a library ladder. She was reaching for a large book. An elderly gentleman stood below, wringing his hands. "Did you find it? Did you find it?" he kept asking.

"That I did," said Trudy. She brushed back the purple curl from her forehead. "But 'finding' and "reaching' are two different things. This book's too high for me." She climbed down. "I'll go ask the custodian to get it down."

"I can help," said Henry. In seconds he climbed the ladder and brought down the book. The gentleman thanked him and hurried off.

Trudy clasped her hands together. "Henry Alden, you're my knight in shining armor." Henry's face turned red. He liked doing things for people, but he was embarrassed when they made a fuss over him. "Now," said Trudy, "what brings my favorite foursome to my library. Oh, I know." She looked at Benny. "You came to research your hundred-day project. Seems like everyone in your class has been here doing research."

Benny looked down at his shoes and shook his head. He still didn't have an idea for his project.

"Actually," said Violet, "we need to research the way Greenfield was a hundred years ago. I remember when I took the library's photography class, you showed us photos from back then."

"Absolutely," said Trudy. "Follow me."

The Aldens had to hurry to keep up. Trudy

entered a room labeled *Archives*. She quickly pulled out old maps, books, photos, and copies of the local newspaper, the *Greenfield Gazette*. The children helped her set everything on one of the big tables. "These items are too old to be in our computer," she said. "Some are fragile, but I know you'll be careful. Call if you need me."

The children worked quietly. They studied everything they could think of to find a Greenfield orphanage. "I sure could use Grandfather's magnifying glass," said Jessie, squinting at an old newspaper. "The type on this page is small and fuzzy."

Violet twisted a pigtail as she searched through photo albums for pictures of an orphanage.

Benny helped Henry carry rolls of maps to a different table. They found a few town maps that were more than one hundred years old. "I can't believe how small Greenfield was back then," said Henry.

"What are these little numbers?" Benny asked. Tiny numbers were printed next to many buildings.

"They help you find the names of the buildings,"

saidHenry. "Look." All down the right side of the map were rows of numbers with names next to them. "This list is called the map's key. It lists the names of important places on this map." Henry pointed to the first name on the key: #1—*City Hall*. "Tryto find number one on the map."

Henry and Benny searched and searched. The numbers on the map were small and hard to find. "This is like my word-find books," said Benny. "Except this is a number find." He kept looking. Suddenly, he saw it. "Here's number one!" he cried. "This is City Hall."

"Great," said Henry. "Try the next one."

Benny looked at the second entry on the key. It said #2—*Fire Station*. Then he searched the map for number two. This time it didn't take long. "Here's the fire station!"

"That's the idea," said Henry. "Now, you take these maps, and I'll take the others. Search the keys for *Orphanage*. Then try to find it on the map."

While Henry and Benny searched, Jessie read through old *Greenfield Gazettes* looking for articles about an orphanage. *Nothing, nothing, nothing.*

And Violet could not find a single photo.

"Orphanage!" cried Benny, pointing to the map. "The key says, 'number seventeen, Orphanage.'"

The others came over and helped search for number seventeen. "There!" said Henry, pointing to a building just outside of town. "There's the orphanage."

"But...but it's not there anymore," said Violet. "That's where they built the Skatium." The children loved skating at the ice rink, which had been around as long as they had lived in Greenfield.

Henry searched the area around the orphanage. There was nothing on the map but a large farm. "Jessie, what did the poem say about a neighbor?"

Jessie recited, "'I hope that this next clue still waits inside my neighbor's friendly gates.'"

Henry tapped his finger on the map. "A hundred years ago, this was the only neighbor anywhere near the orphanage." The number twenty-two was written on a building. Henry looked at the map key. "The building used to be called Daisy's Dairy Farm!"

"The dairy's still there!" said Benny. "My class

went there on a field trip. I got to milk a cow."

"Well, then," said Henry, smiling, "we'd better get MOO-ving."

MOO-ving Day

The Aldens made a quick stop at home for lunch. The kitchen became a flurry of sandwich making. Mrs. McGregor's sandwiches would have been tidier, but the children's sandwiches would taste almost as delicious. And Mrs. McGregor would *never* have thought to put sweet-pickle slices inside Benny's peanut butter and jelly sandwich. They brought their creations to the kitchen table and started eating.

The metal box with *The Only* sat in the center of the table. "Let's bring this book to Wintham Manor," Jessie said. "A famous one-hundred-fifty-year-old book might help Ella bring visitors to the manor."

MOO-ving Day

"I've been thinking a lot about the manor," said Henry. "I've always dreamed about building my own house someday. And I've studied every book of house plans in the library. But I've never seen anything built like the manor. Why did Alfred Wintham build it that way? I can't figure out what he was thinking."

Violet speared a pickle from the jar. "I've never been inside a more fun house," she said. "We can't let them tear it down. We just can't!"

Jessie passed around a bowl of fresh berries. "I'm really curious about who wrote the *Journal for the Curious*," she said. "A hundred years ago, the writer created a wild treasure hunt. But why?"

"Jessie, you should blog about our search for the treasure," said Violet. "People love treasure hunts."

Jessie thought about the idea. Her *Where in Greenfield?* blog had started as a project for her computer class. At first, only her classmates had read it. But then the *Greenfield Gazette* ran an article about her school's "Brilliant, Budding Bloggers." Suddenly, a few *hundred* fans were following Jessie's blog.

"All my readers love solving riddles," said Jessie. "I'll blog the clues we've been following. My readers can try to guess where we've been."

"They'll never guess," said Benny, his lips and tongue blue from eating blueberries. "Not in a million, billion, kazillion years."

"You can use my pictures," said Violet. She picked up her camera and went back through the photos she'd taken. "Here's one of Henry pulling the time capsule out of the cornerstone. And here's the *Journal for the Curious*."

"I'll post your photos tonight with the first clue." Jessie held the journal steady while Violet took a photo of the clue.

Jessie turned the page. "Tomorrow, I'll post your photo of the finger rocks. I'll show the box with *The Only* inside. Then I'll give my readers the second clue." Violet photographed the second clue.

Jessie's voice grew more excited as she planned her blogs. "And the next day I'll post the photo of the old map that shows the orphanage and—"

"Daisy's Dairy," said Henry. He checked his watch. "It's getting late. We have to go to the dairy.

We'd better get..." He paused and smiled. "I said, *we'd better get...*"

"MOOOOO-ving!" the others said together.

***

The children biked past the Skatium ice rink, where the orphanage used to be. Soon they rode along a wood fence. It curved around pastures as far as they could see. Cows grazed in the fields or sat in the shade of trees. A large sign at the dairy entrance said:

Daisy's Dairy
Delicious milk from happy cows
Visit our stand for fresh milk, cheese, butter,
yogurt, ice cream, milkshakes
Open 10-4 Daily

"Ice cream!" cried Benny, pedaling past the others. Even after a big lunch, Benny always had room for ice cream.

The farm stand stood next to a large white farmhouse. A woman was placing different kinds of cheeses into a glass case. Another case displayed many flavors of ice cream. Benny pressed his nose against the glass. There were so many flavors. He wished he could bring one hundred ice-cream cones for his hundred-day project.

"Howdy," said the woman, wiping her hands on her apron. "I'm Anabel. What can I get for you?" She had a kind smile and cheerful voice.

"A chocolate cone, please," said Benny.

"Comin' right up." Anabel picked up a colorful cane and walked behind the counter. She rested the cane to one side while she scooped their orders.

As she handed Henry his strawberry cone, he asked, "Do you know if someone named Tyler used to live here?"

Anabel's eyebrows shot up in surprise. "Tyler? Wh...why, he was my grandfather. But he died years ago. How do you know his name?"

"It's in a poem we found," said Jessie. "A riddle. The person who wrote it lived in an orphanage that used to be next door to your farm. Your grandfather Tyler was his friend."

"Well, I'll be gobsmacked," said Anabel. She handed Violet a vanilla cone. "I have heard stories

about that orphanage, but it was gone before I was born."

Benny licked around the sides of his cone. "Do you remember your grandfather?" he asked.

"Oh, I was just a little tyke when he died," said Anabel. "All I have left of Grandpa Tyler is some old stuff in the attic—war medals, a bunch of old photos, that sort of thing."

A car pulled up. Anabel waved as four noisy children piled out of the car and raced toward the stand.

"Just one more thing," said Jessie. "Could you tell us if this makes sense to you?" Jessie recited:

> *I hope that this next clue still waits*
> *Inside my neighbor's friendly gates*
> *I asked that Tyler please pass down, my*
> *Brownie treats that caught our town*

"We thought your Grandpa Tyler might have passed down a brownie recipe or something," said Henry.

Anabel's smile disappeared. Her soft voice grew sharp. "Brownies? Why on earth would we have brownies? We're a dairy farm not a bakery. Now, if you'll excuse me, I have customers to tend to."

"But—" Benny started to say.

Henry put a hand on Benny's shoulder. "Let's go."

***

The next morning, the children sat quietly around

the breakfast table. Benny rested his elbows on the table. He propped his chin on his hands and stared at the writing on the back of the Panquake box. He was trying to read all the words. Watch sat next to the stove, his tail wagging as Grandfather heaped pancakes on a platter. James Alden was concerned. It wasn't like his grandchildren to be so quiet in the morning. He carried the pancakes to the table.

"I know the Panquake box says to 'just add water,'" said Grandfather. "But it doesn't say 'don't add blueberries.'" He set down pancakes that seemed as much blueberries as pancake.

The children perked up at the taste of plump berries inside warm pancakes. They told Grandfather about their trip to Daisy's Dairy.

"The woman, Anabel, was really nice," said Violet, "until Jessie told her the riddle."

"Hmm," said Grandfather. "I wonder why. May I see the poem again?" Jessie brought him the journal. He read the riddle a few times. "I see nothing in these words to upset someone. Did you ask her about these 'Brownie treats'?"

Jessie nodded. "That's when she got upset."

The Hundred-Year Mystery

After breakfast, Grandfather left to run errands. Henry, Violet, and Benny cleaned up. Jessie stayed at the table, staring at the poem. She liked reading poems, but something about the words in this one seemed strange.

> *I asked that Tyler please pass down, my*
> *Brownie treats that caught our town*

Finally, she saw it. "Look," she said. "This poem is written wrong." She pointed to the words *down* and *town*. "These are the two words that rhyme. They should be at the end of each line."

Jessie wrote out the lines on a sheet of paper.

> *I asked that Tyler please pass* **down**
> *My brownie treats that caught our* **town**

Violet looked at the two poems. "It looks like the author wrote the poem to make *Brownie* the first word of the line."

Henry nodded. "I see what you are saying. He wanted the *B* capitalized. Why would he do that?"

"It has to be the name of something," said Jessie.

"Brownie," Violet whispered, "Brownie, Brownie, Brownie..." It sounded familiar. But what sort of Brownie could capture a town?

"Brownie could be a nickname if the person's last name was Brown," said Henry.

"Or," said Benny, looking at the box of pancake mix, "it could be the name of a brand. Like the *P* in *Panquake*."

"That's it!" cried Violet, clapping her hands. "Brownie is a type of camera. My photography teacher brought a Brownie to class. It was over a hundred years old!"

Henry shook his head. "The Brownie in our poem can't mean a camera."

Violet's smile disappeared. "Why not?" she asked.

"Remember when we lived in the boxcar?" said Henry. "We earned money by mowing lawns and walking dogs and working in gardens. Every penny we earned went to buy food. We could never afford anything as expensive as a camera."

Violet's smile came back. "But that's what made the Brownie camera famous! It was made out of cardboard. It only cost a dollar."

Jessie slapped her hand on the table. "Now the poem makes sense. 'Brownie treats' aren't food. They are photos the orphan boy took of Greenfield. Photos 'that caught our town.'"

Violet gasped. "Anabel said she has her Grandpa Tyler's photos in the attic." Her voice dropped to a whisper. "I wonder if she still has his Brownie camera."

"That settles it," said Henry. "We have to go back to Daisy's Dairy."

Benny's eyes grew wide. "B...but what if Anabel is mean again?"

"We can't stop now," said Henry. "We might be close to finding the treasure."

"And Ella is counting on us," said Jessie. "We have to find the treasure to help save Wintham Manor."

Secrets in the Attic

Henry rang the doorbell of the white farmhouse. It chimed "Old McDonald Had a Farm." The children heard Anabel's cane clacking on the floor. Benny hid behind Henry and peeked out as the door opened.

Anabel looked surprised. "Oh," she said, "it's you." She did not sound angry. "I was hoping you would come back. I feel bad about the way I acted yesterday. Please, come in."

The children looked at each other. This wasn't the greeting they had expected. Inside, the house smelled like Mrs. McGregor's home cooking. The Aldens followed Anabel into a sunny yellow kitchen. "I'm fixing lunch for the farmworkers," she said.

She stopped to stir a large pot. "Please, sit down."

The children sat at a large, round table. "Why did you hope we'd come back?" asked Jessie.

"Because I want to apologize," Anabel said, joining them at the table. "You surprised me yesterday. I hadn't heard Grandpa Tyler's name in years and years." She brushed back a strand of hair. "And when you mentioned the Brownie..." Anabel pressed her lips together. She looked like she might cry. "I knew right away you meant his old Brownie camera."

"May we see it?" asked Violet.

Anabel looked even sadder. "It's gone," she said. A tear rolled down her cheek. "I sold it." She took a tissue from her apron pocket and blew her nose. "We were having a yard sale a few years back, getting rid of all sorts of old things. I was clearing the attic when I found the Brownie in a chest with Grandpa's photos. That old Brownie was nothing more than a cardboard box with a little lens put in. I offered it to my kids and grandkids, but they'd rather take photos with their cell phones. So..." Anabel sighed. "I set the Brownie out at the yard sale, and someone bought it." She wiped her hands on her apron. "I always felt bad about selling something that belonged to Grandpa Tyler." She smiled at the children. "I wasn't mad at you. I was upset with myself."

Violet's stomach did a little flip. Had they lost their next clue? "Was...was there film in the Brownie when you sold it?" she asked.

"No," said Anabel, "I checked."

"Whew," said Violet. "That's good. That means your grandpa Tyler developed all the pictures in the camera."

"Well, there's plenty of photos up in that old chest." The kitchen timer dinged, and Anabel pushed up from the table. "You're more than welcome to go to the attic and take a look-see."

The children ran to the attic. The room was almost too hot to breathe in. Henry tried opening windows, but they were painted shut. A light bulb hung down from a thick cord in the middle of the attic. Jessie pulled the chain, and the room lit up. "Oh dear," she said. The attic was full of old furniture, magazines, and racks of clothing. There were boxes everywhere.

Jessie shook her head. "I wonder what this attic looked like before the yard sale."

"There's so much stuff," said Violet. "We'll never find the photos."

"Anabel said the photos would be in a chest," said Henry. "Let's start with those."

The Aldens spread out in four different directions, climbing over and under, looking through all sorts of things. Benny called, "This chest has someone's soda can collection. Maybe I can bring a hundred soda cans to school for my project."

"Keep looking for photos," said Henry.

Jessie opened a chest that smelled like mothballs. There was an old army uniform inside. Violet found a chest of holiday decorations.

"I think I found it!" called Henry. He stood over a small chest filled with stacks of black-and-white photos. They were in neat bundles tied with twine. He slid out a photo of two boys. The words *Tyler and* AJ were written on the back. Henry lifted the chest onto his shoulder.

"Where are you going?" asked Benny.

"Back down where it's cool," said Henry.

Secrets in the Attic

***

"Set that right here," said Anabel. Henry put the chest on the kitchen table and opened it. Each stack of photos had a piece of paper on top with a date. Henry lifted out a stack marked *AJ and ME*. "I never heard tell of any AJ," said Anabel.

The pictures showed two boys. Henry took out a photo of a husky boy with straight blond hair. The boy, who looked about Henry's age, stood on a small bridge holding a fishing pole. Anabel smiled. "That's Grandpa Tyler, all right. All the men in our family look just like that." In another photo, a boy with curly dark hair sat on a black-and-white cow. The boy was smiling and waving at the camera. AJ was written on the back of the photo.

There was a photo of the boys leaning against a Welcome to Greenfield sign. There were photos of them licking lollipops in front of The Penny Candy Shoppe, of them watching a blacksmith shoe a horse, and of them using sticks to roll metal hoops down the street. In the background, there were horses and wagons, women in long dresses, and men in suits and hats. Horses pulled wagons down the street. "Where are all the cars?" asked Benny.

"There weren't many back then," said Anabel. "Too expensive. Most people walked or biked or took a horse." She pushed up from the table to check her cooking.

Violet held up a photo and laughed. "Look at this one." It was taken on Greenfield's Main Street. A big stone container sat on a street corner. Water flowed into it from a spout. In the photo, Tyler and AJ bent over the container and pretended to drink the water. A horse drank next to them.

"Eee-yeww!" Jessie wrinkled her nose. "I hope those boys didn't *really* drink that water. Eee-yeww!"

The children spread out the photos: AJ and Tyler shooting marbles. AJ and Tyler swimming in a pond. AJ and Tyler fishing.

"You can just tell they were best friends," said Henry.

Violet pointed to a few photos. "Look," she said. "Tyler wears all sorts of different clothes. But AJ always wears the same dark pants and long socks."

Henry pulled out other photos of AJ. In some

backgrounds there were other boys dressed like him. Henry slapped the photos on the table, one by one. *Slap.* "AJ's wearing a uniform." *Slap.* "AJ lived in the orphanage next door." *Slap.* "It's AJ's journal we've been reading!"

The Aldens stared at the photos. At last, here was the face of the orphan whose clues had led them this far.

"Those orphan boys didn't have much," said Anabel. "My aunt told me those boys were fed and kept safe. Young ones, maybe Benny's age, cleaned the orphanage and tended the garden. The bigger boys found jobs in town. I don't think they had much time for play." She shook her head. "Years back I saw pictures of the inside of the orphanage. Not a speck of fun anywhere in that place." She picked up a photo of AJ jumping from a tire swing into a pond. "AJ was lucky to make a good friend like Grandpa Tyler. And I reckon Grandpa Tyler was lucky to have AJ too." She smiled at the photo of the two friends. "I wonder what ever became of AJ."

"We think he was a builder," said Henry. "Maybe a stonemason or a construction worker." They told her about Wintham Manor and the cornerstone and the hundred-year-old journal they'd found. "We've been following AJ's clues. They're supposed to lead to a treasure."

"A treasure!" Anabel laughed with delight. "Imagine Grandpa Tyler having a best friend who had a *treasure*."

"May we borrow some of these photos?" asked

Violet. "We promise to return them."

"It's the least I can do after the sorry way I treated you yesterday." Anabel slipped the photos into a plastic bag and gave them to Violet. "Just promise to let me know what treasure you find."

***

Outside, Jessie opened the journal to the next clue.

> *We "caught," as you now plainly see,*
> *How we had fun when we were free*
> *But Ty and I could never play*
> *Before our work was done each day*
>
> *At early morn—in heat and cold—*
> *I earned my keep with papers sold*
> *I hawked the news of town and nation*
> *Near the Main Street "filling station"*

"AJ sold newspapers?" said Henry. "He was a paperboy like me?" Henry had a morning paper route delivering the *Greenfield Gazette*.

"Except," said Jessie, "you deliver the newspapers by bike. This clue says AJ was 'hawking news.'"

"A hawk? He used big birds to carry the newspapers?" Benny asked.

Jessie smiled. "It would be fun to have an eagle deliver our paper. But what AJ means when he says 'I hawked the news' is that he stood outside and yelled the headlines to try to get people to buy newspapers."

"Like the paperboys in those old movies Grandfather watches," Benny said. He pretended to hold up a newspaper. Then he strutted around calling, "Ex-tra! Ex-tra! Read all about it!" He looked so funny they all started laughing. A couple of cows in the pasture turned to look.

Henry said, "You're going to make a great paperboy." He climbed onto his bike.

"Where are we going?" asked Benny.

"To the Main Street filling station," said Henry.

"What's that?" asked Violet.

"It's an old-fashioned name for a gas station," said Henry. "And there's only one gas station on Main Street."

The Paperboy's Clue

Gus's Gas Station stood on the corner of Main Street and Tucker Avenue. The children found Gus working under the hood of a truck. The cheerful man often fixed Grandfather's car, and he always invited Henry to watch.

"When did the first gas station open in Greenfield?" Henry asked.

Gus chuckled. "Now there's a question I don't hear every day." He wiped his hands on his work rag. "I guess it would be when my grandpa Gus opened this place about eighty years ago."

"But it needs to be a hundred years ago," said Benny.

Gus squinted one eye, thinking. "Nope," he said.

"Sorry, Benny. A hundred years ago, cars were a pretty new invention. They were expensive and always breaking down. Greenfield was mostly farmland back then, and farmers used horses to get around. There wouldn't have been gas stations in town."

"But a few people must have owned cars," said Henry. "Where would they buy gas?"

"Oh, they'd probably drive over to a bigger town like Elmford," Gus said. "There'd be more cars there needing a fill-up."

The smell of hamburgers drifted by. Benny's stomach rumbled. "I need a fill-up," he said.

"You're in luck," said Gus. "My wife's barbecuing in the lot next door."

Cook's Corner was a big metal grill set up along the Main Street sidewalk. The chalkboard menu listed hot dogs, hamburgers, and corn on the cob. A few picnic tables with umbrellas were set around the lot. At the grill, a woman in a chef's hat chatted with customers. The Aldens quickly checked their money. They had enough for each of them to have a nice big ear of corn. Benny watched as the corn grilled. "I could bring a hundred ears of corn for my hundred-day project," he said.

Henry ruffled Benny's hair. "I don't think you have enough money for that idea. You'll come up with something though. Keep trying."

Honk! Honk! The yellow Levi's Lumber truck pulled up to the curb. Circles of tree trunk filled the back of the truck like giant checkers. Levi climbed out. "Want to see what the inside of a giant tree looks like?"

"I do!" said Benny, running over. Levi lifted him up to look at the pieces of wood. Each slice had circles inside. The circle at the center was the smallest. The one around it was bigger. The one around that was bigger still. The Aldens gathered around.

"These rings are sort of like the candles on your birthday cake," said Levi. "Candles show how old you are. A tree grows a ring every year to show how old it is." Benny reached out and touched the rings. Then Levi set Benny down. "I'm dropping these at the furniture maker," he said, climbing back into his truck. "I'll be cutting more circles in a little while. Come watch if you're out near Wintham

Manor." He waved as he drove away.

"I'd like to see him cut the tree," Benny said.

"It would be interesting," Henry said. "But what about finding the treasure?"

"Oh," said Benny, "I want to do that too!"

"First things, first," said Jessie. They took their corn to a table along Main Street. "First we eat, then we look for the next clue, then we try to see Levi cutting up the tree."

The children began pulling the husks off their ears of corn. Jessie peeled hers slowly, thinking. This riddle seemed so much harder than the others. "If there wasn't a gas station on Main Street a hundred years ago," she said, "what could the Main Street 'filling station' be?"

"We're filling up with corn," said Benny. "Maybe it was a restaurant."

They began eating as they tried to solve the riddle. Jessie always ate her corn straight across— neatly biting two rows at a time. When she finished, not a single niblet was left on the cob. Henry turned his cob round and round, eating in circles. Violet bit her corn into V's. And Benny ate his corn every which way until the cob and his face were a very big mess.

Jessie finished and set her corn aside. "Maybe it will help to go through the clues." She took out the journal and turned to the first clue. "So far, every one of AJ's riddles gave us the information we needed."

Go to where the sun's first ray
Shines just east of town each day

"We did that," said Jessie. "We found that tall finger rock that Henry climbed."

Then plumb a line both straight and true
And dig there for your second clue

"Henry dropped down the horseshoe on a string," said Jessie. "We dug up the book AJ buried—*The Only*. That's how we found out he was an orphan. And that led us to the library to find where Greenfield's orphanage was."

She looked at the next clue.

The Hundred-Year Mystery

I hope that this next clue still waits
Inside my neighbor's friendly gates
I asked that Tyler please pass down, my
Brownie treats that caught our town

"The 'neighbor's friendly gates' was Daisy's Dairy, where Tyler lived. In the attic, we found the chest with AJ and Tyler's photos of our town—their 'Brownie treats.'" Jessie sighed. "But we can't figure out this next part."

Hawking news of town and nation
Near the Main Street "filling station"

Violet took AJ's photos from her backpack. Main Street looked so different back then. Now the street was paved and wider. It had bright streetlamps and new stores and cars instead of horses. A large round planter full of flowers stood in front. She stared at one photo, then looked across the street at a redbrick building. "Look," she said, "the *Greenfield Gazette* building is still on the same corner it was a hundred years ago."

The Paperboy's Clue

"That's where I pick up the newspapers for my paper route," said Henry. "I wonder if that's where AJ sold his newspapers."

Jessie looked at the photo, then at the building. "The *Gazette* looks the same," she said, "except there's no flower planter in AJ's photo. There's just a water fountain."

Henry looked at the photo then at the *Greenfield Gazette*. "Hold on, hold on," he said, quickly shuffling through the pile of AJ's photos. He pulled out the photo of AJ and Tyler pretending to drink from the horse's watering trough. Then he looked across the street. "I think I found our filling station!"

***

Henry reached the planter first. He lifted the leafy vines aside. Violet gasped. "It's the same trough!"

Henry smiled. "Welcome to AJ's Main Street filling station," he said. "This is where horses *filled up* with water."

Benny let out a whoop and galloped around, pretending to be a horse. "We did the trick. We did the trick. I can't believe we did the trick!"

Violet ran her fingers along the stone. "A hundred years ago," she said softly, "AJ touched this exact same trough."

Henry pictured AJ standing right here. "A hundred years ago," he said, "AJ sold newspapers on this corner."

The children grew quiet. "I feel like AJ is one of us," said Violet. "An orphan like us whose journal brought us here. Where does he want us to go next?"

Jessie opened the journal and said, "This is his last clue." Then she read out loud:

At eighteen years I left my home
The North, South, East, and West to roam
While selling those which I loved best
Before returning here to nest

'Twas then I thought that I might dare
Create a way, my love to share
I bound my passion and my pleasure
Into types of golden treasure

"Gold! Treasure!" cried Benny.

The Paperboy's Clue

"Hush," said Violet. "Listen."

Jessie continued:

> *Now follow where these waters flow*
> *A milestone to the east will show*
> *A backward way to reach the hope*
> *Awaiting at my climbing rope*
>
> *Once up, just turn, and you will see*
> *My treasure trove imPRESSing thee*

Violet could not understand what all the words meant. The poem had so many ideas and mysteries all at one time. But one phrase did sound very beautiful. "How can we 'follow where these waters flow'?" she asked. "There is no river here, no creek."

Henry lifted more vines aside. A rusty spout stuck out. "This is how water flowed into the trough. If too much water filled the trough, it would flow over the sides and run downhill." Henry looked up and down Main Street and pointed. "This road goes downhill to the east. That's the way we need to ride."

The excited children ran to the corner. The stoplight was green, and cars whizzed past. The Aldens waited. And waited. It seemed the light would never turn red so they could walk. "The poem said 'milestone,'" said Benny. "What's a milestone?"

Jessie thought. "Well, it can be a really important moment in your life. Like your first day of school. Or when you learned to ride a two-wheeler. Those were milestones."

"But sometimes," said Henry, "a milestone is a *real* stone or flag or something that marks one mile. Like the flags along the three-mile race I ran last week."

Finally, the light changed, and they ran to their bikes.

***

Henry's compass led the children east out of town. In the distance, the fingerlike rocks reached for the sky. Soon, the children pulled up to the rocks and stopped.

"Could this be the milestone?" asked Benny.

Henry bit his lower lip, thinking. "No, we're more than a mile from town."

The Paperboy's Clue

Benny remembered the first time he'd come here. The others had ridden far ahead of him. He'd stopped to look at the rocks. "I saw some weird writing on this stone." Benny bent down and pointed to the markings near the bottom of the tallest rock. "But I can't read it."

Violet studied the stone and said, "Jessie, say the clue again."

Jessie read from the journal:

> *Now follow where these waters flow*
> *A milestone to the east will show*
> *A backward way to reach the hope*
> *Awaiting at my climbing rope*

Suddenly, Violet rolled her bike off the path and over to the tallest finger. She turned the bike so that it was facing away from the rock. Then she sat down on the seat and adjusted the mirror on her handlebars.

Jessie laughed. "You look like you're taking a selfie."

Violet jumped up. "Try it!" Jessie quickly sat

down on Violet's bike. She tilted the mirror so she could see the strange letters behind her. But when she looked at the letters in the mirror, they weren't strange at all. Henry and Benny tried it too.

"That's called mirror writing," said Violet. "The writing is backward unless you look at it in a mirror."

The Paperboy's Clue

In the mirror, the backward letters said *1MILETOAJWM.*

"This is the milestone in the clue!" said Henry. "It doesn't mean one mile *from* town. It means one mile *to* someplace."

"Someplace called AJWM," said Jessie.

"What's one mile away from here?" Benny asked, looking all around.

They thought of where they had ridden their bikes the first time they passed these rocks. And, suddenly, every one of them knew exactly what was one mile away.

"It's one mile to AJWM," said Henry. "AJ Wintham's Manor."

Now they knew who hid the capsule in the cornerstone.

"AJ wasn't a stonemason who laid the cornerstone," said Jessie.

"He wasn't a construction worker who helped build the manor," said Henry.

"AJ was Alfred J. Wintham!" said Benny. "And his treasure is waiting for us at AJ's house— Wintham Manor!"

AJ's Treasure

Ella opened the manor door and the Aldens burst in, all talking at once. "Mr. Wintham wrote the journal!" "He's AJ!" "He carved a backward clue on a rock!"

Ella's head turned from one child to the other. Her silky hair swished as she tried to keep up. Laughing, she held up her hands and said, "Hold on, hold on. One at a time."

The children explained how they followed the clues in AJ's journal. "All the riddles lead back to this manor," said Henry.

Benny could hardly sit still. "The treasure is here!"

"Are you sure?" asked Ella. "How can that be?"

"You know the manor better than anyone," Jessie said. "Can you think where a treasure might be hidden?"

Ella tapped a finger against her lips. "Hmm," she said. "Hmm. The only part of the manor I've never seen is high up in the tower."

"Rapunzel's tower?" asked Violet.

"That must be where the treasure is," said Benny. "It *must* be! But...but the rope ladder is gone. How can we climb up?"

"There's a ladder in the basement," Ella said. She took the children downstairs, but the ladder was too small to reach the beam high in the tower. They searched for rope they could knot into a ladder. But all Ella had was a ball of kitchen twine and some fuzzy knitting yarn.

Whirrrr. Bzzzzzz. Whirrr. The sound of Levi's chain saw startled them. "That's it!" said Jessie. "I know how we'll climb up into the tower."

***

Circles of tree trunk lay all around the yard. *Whirrrr. Bzzzzzz.* Levi had almost finished cutting the old tree trunk into slices. He looked surprised to see Ella and the Alden children rushing toward him. He was even more surprised when they told him what they needed.

Levi went to his truck and took out a small ladder. "That ladder will never reach the top of the tower," said Violet. "We need the tall ladder you used when you cut down the tree."

"Well then," said Levi, "we'd better use some magic." He wiggled his fingers over the ladder and said, "Abracadabra, hocus-pocus!" And, with that, he gripped the top step of the little ladder and pulled. The ladder grew longer and longer. It would reach very high.

"My telescope slides open like that," said Henry.

Levi grinned. "That's why they call this a 'telescoping ladder.'" He closed the ladder and said, "Lead the way."

The excited group hurried up the staircase and into the twisty attic rooms. Levi could barely squeeze through the low doorways and narrow passages. Finally, they reached the tower.

Levi expanded the telescoping ladder. It went up and up and up. Finally, it reached the beam where the rope ladder used to be. Levi rested the ladder against the beam. He leaned his weight against it to make sure it would hold firm.

"Okay," he said, "who's climbing?"

Four hands flew up. "We all climb trees in our backyard," explained Henry.

Henry started, and the others followed. One by one they reached the platform that circled around the high tower. A strong metal railing ran all around. Carefully, each child stepped off the ladder onto the platform. Hundred-year-old dust swirled around their feet.

"Look," said Jessie, pointing across the tower. "Rapunzel's window. You can see all of Greenfield from here."

"Ohhh," said Violet, "that's the view AJ painted on the mural downstairs."

"And it's also like the view from the top of the rock," Henry said, "where he read his books."

Ella called up to them, "Did you find anything?"

"Not yet," said Henry. He turned to Jessie. "What did the clue say?"

Jessie recited, "'Once up, just turn, and you will

see my treasure trove imPRESSing thee.'"

The children turned. There was nothing up here but the walkway. All the walls were brick. Violet held on to the railing and walked around the platform. She noticed a rectangle of bricks darker than the others. She thought, *My treasure trove imPRESSing thee.* Violet pressed against the dark bricks. Nothing happened. She pressed again. Still nothing. The others came to help. All four children pressed together. A brick door swung open. They jumped back.

It was black as night inside. The air smelled of dust and age. The only light came from the doorway.

Benny stepped back. "I don't want to go in," he said.

"Let's wait until our eyes adjust to the dark," said Henry. After a minute, they could see a small table in the middle of a small room.

"Look," whispered Violet. A large brass capsule sat on the table. "It's like the one in the cornerstone."

Henry darted into the dark room and brought out the capsule. He unscrewed the gray cap and took out a piece of paper.

"What is it?" asked Jessie.

Henry squinted. "It looks like a letter," he said. "But it's too dark up here. Let's take it downstairs."

***

Everyone sat around the kitchen table as Henry read the letter written in AJ's fancy writing.

Dear Curious Ones,

Congratulations! You solved my journal's riddles that led you back here to my home. I hope you enjoyed your trip through my world as it was a hundred years ago. As I write this, a few people in Greenfield have begun traveling in automobiles. Some people light their homes with electricity instead of candles and gaslight. And people have begun putting telephones in their homes. These are exciting times! Oh, how I wish I could see what your world looks like. I imagine it is quite wonderful.

But now, let me answer the biggest riddle of all. How did an orphan like me with empty pockets and an emptier stomach come to build such a grand manor? I had very little when I was young. But books swept me away to amazing places. I traveled to Mars, China, and Africa. I sailed mighty ships and flew daredevil airplanes and dove to the bottom of the sea—all without ever leaving the top of my reading rock, my "home away from home."

To be happy, I believe you should do what you love most. I loved books most! When I left the orphanage, I earned money by selling books door-to-door. After a few years, I began making books of my own. Writers sent me stories. Illustrators sent me drawings. And at AJ Wintham & Company, we made these into magical books. I worked hard at publishing. In time, I grew wealthy and wanted to share my good fortune. So I returned to

AJ's Treasure

Greenfield and built Wintham Manor to be a magical, joyful, safe place for all children...to play, to create, to read.

Now that you've followed the journal's clues to my home, can you guess what my treasure is?

Your friend,
Alfred J. Wintham

Henry put the letter on the table. "No wonder we have so much fun here. AJ built this house for kids!"

"Does that mean this house is his treasure?" asked Benny.

Jessie shook her head. "I don't think so." She took out AJ's journal and turned back to the final riddle.

> *'Twas then I thought that I might dare*
> *Create a way, my love to share*
> *I bound my passion and my pleasure*
> *Into types of golden treasure*

"Types of golden treasure," said Jessie. "That doesn't sound like the manor. I think the treasure is still upstairs!"

This time the children brought flashlights. They climbed the ladder and entered the room where they'd found the capsule. They flashed their flashlights all around.

"A door!" Benny cried. He pulled it open, and they all stepped inside. Books! Shelves and shelves of books lined the walls.

"No wonder the tower looks so big outside but so small inside," said Violet. "AJ built his secret library between the two walls."

The Aldens followed the space that curved all around the tower. There were baby books, picture books, chapter books, teen books, scary books, silly books—all for children. *Alfred J. Wintham* was printed on the spine of every single one. "AJ's company published all of these," said Violet.

"That's the answer!" said Jessie. "When AJ wrote about '*types* of golden treasure,' he meant the words *typed* on the pages of these books. These books are his treasure."

"We found it!" whooped Benny.

Violet laughed. "We sure did!"

"One hundred years," said Henry, high-fiving them all, "and nobody found it but us." He ran ahead to see what else he could find.

Violet pulled a beautiful picture book off the shelf. "Maybe someday I'll illustrate a book like this."

Next to her, Jessie paged through a mystery. "Maybe someday I'll write one."

"Here's more!" Henry carried in big rolls of papers and unrolled them on the floor. Their four flashlights shone on AJ's drawings. One showed children sliding down zigzaggy slides. Another showed children painting on the art room walls. A third showed children snuggled in comfy reading rooms. "These drawings look like plans for the manor!"

Benny ran back out to the railing and yelled, "We found AJ's treasure!" He whooped again and again. His cheers echoed around and around Rapunzel's tower and floated out the window toward town.

The children raced down the stairs and gave the plans to Ella. They told her about the treasure trove of books and showed her AJ's drawings.

"You did it!" said Ella. "You children solved the mystery of Wintham Manor. I never thought I would see the day..." She wiped away happy tears. "Now I understand the low doorways and all the fun rooms and the twisty attic. AJ built this manor to be a children's club, a place where all children could come—no matter what their background."

"Like a home away from home," said Jessie.

Violet thought back to the story of the flu epidemic that had gone through Greenfield. "AJ must have passed away before he told anyone his dream," she said. "That's so sad."

Ella took a deep breath. She lifted her chin and set her shoulders back. "AJ's story may have a happy ending yet," she said, her voice determined. "If you'll excuse me, I have a phone call to make."

The children left Ella to make her phone call and started on their way home. As they were leaving the manor, Levi's yellow truck rattled past. The back was piled high with slices of tree.

Suddenly, Benny started pedaling after the truck. "Wait! Wait!" he called. For several minutes the big man and small boy had a very serious talk. Then Levi drove away.

"What was that all about?" asked Henry.

"You were right, Henry," said Benny. "Our hunt for AJ's treasure made me forget all about my problem, and the answer snuck right up on me!"

***

COUNT THE RINGS ON 100-YEAR-OLD TREE

The Hundred-Year Mystery

At school the next week, crowds of families and friends came to see the students' hundred-day projects. Booths and tables were set up all around the schoolyard. And, leaning against the fence, was a big round slice of tree. Benny proudly stood next to it. He'd written a sign:

COUNT THE RINGS ON 100-YEAR-OLD TREE.

He gave people Grandfather's magnifying glass to help count the rings.

Taped to the tree was a big blue ribbon: "First Prize—Most Original Hundred-Day Project."

The Fight for the Manor

When the hundred-day project was over, Levi brought Benny's slice of tree to the Aldens' house. Henry helped him set it on top of the small red table next to the house. Now the children had a big table for their picnics and projects. Violet drew a thank-you card for Levi that all the children signed.

The first morning of summer vacation, Ella called, excited. "The mayor just called!" she said. "She wants to meet with Levi and me in three days. She wants us to tell her why we think Wintham Manor should not be torn down. We're bringing the drawings you found in the attic. And we'll show her the *Journal for the Curious* and *The Only* and photos of AJ's books. Everything, everything,

everything!" Ella promised to call the children just as soon as the meeting was over.

At first, the children were excited. But then Violet's lip began to quiver. "What if the mayor says no? I can't bear to think of the manor being torn down."

"It's the funnest house ever!" said Benny.

Henry started pacing back and forth. "We can't just sit around doing nothing," he said. "We need to help."

"We can make a flyer about AJ and the manor," said Violet. She quickly brought out drawing paper and colored pencils. "We'll ask everyone in Greenfield to call the mayor and tell her not to close the manor. I can put in a photo of AJ and one of Wintham Manor." She began drawing.

Henry paced some more. He snapped his fingers. "The *Gazette* is always looking for a good story. I'll tell them AJ was a paperboy for the *Gazette* a hundred years ago. I'll tell them about his dream for Wintham Manor. Maybe the *Gazette* will let me and all the other kids put flyers in our newspaper deliveries." He turned to Violet. "As soon as you finish the flyer," he said, "I'll bike over to the *Gazette* and show it to them."

"I'll carry flyers to stores in my wagon," Benny said, "like we do for our yard sales."

Jessie had a different idea. She ran to the computer. Her *Where in Greenfield?* blog filled the screen. Her readers were having fun trying to solve AJ's riddles. They had written to Jessie saying: "We found the tall finger rock!" "We found the horse watering trough!" "We ate ice cream at Daisy's Dairy!"

Now Jessie typed about AJ's dream of a special place for children. At the end of her blog, she wrote "Please help save Wintham Manor." She typed the mayor's email address and phone number in great big letters and wrote "Write or call before it's too late!" Then she pressed Send. In seconds, her blog went out to her readers all across Greenfield.

The next day, the *Gazette* published a story about the Alden's adventure. The newspaper editor liked Henry's story so much, he printed the flyers for free. Every copy of the *Greenfield Gazette* was delivered with a brightly colored flyer inside.

The Hundred-Year Mystery

Flyers appeared in store windows all across town. Suddenly, everyone in Greenfield was talking about saving Wintham Manor.

Three days later, Ella called the Aldens with the good news. "They're not tearing down Wintham Manor!" she said. "They're going to turn it into the children's club AJ dreamed about. And, thanks to all of you, many people and businesses are donating money. Lots and lots of money. You saved Wintham Manor!"

***

For weeks the children were not allowed to go to the manor. "It's too dangerous," explained Ella. "There are carpenters, plumbers, painters, and electricians working everywhere. Levi is showing all the workers exactly what to do. *AJ's Place*— that's what we're calling it—is looking grand. Just the way AJ wanted it."

Finally, one day, Ella called. "We're having our grand opening this weekend. I would like you all to come the day before for a special tour."

As the children neared the manor, they hardly recognized it. The dirty stone building had been scrubbed clean. Dark trim around the windows now shone white as the clouds. In front, colorful mobiles turned in the breeze. Hopscotch squares, dot-to-dot pictures, tic-tac-toe grids, and other games were painted on the sidewalk. Someone had written "Welcome to AJ's Place!" in sidewalk chalk.

Henry banged the heavy door knocker. The sound echoed through the house. Benny remembered when he first came here. When he was afraid there were ghosts. That seemed like a very long time ago. "Coming, COME-ing," called Ella's singsong voice. "Hold your horses. Hoooold your horses." Slowly, the door swung open. Ella wore jeans and a T-shirt that said "AJ's Place."

Inside, the manor looked the same, but different. The doorways were still kid-size. Alfred Wintham's mural of Greenfield still decorated the entrance wall. But the rooms seemed brighter. The furniture newer. The Aldens followed Ella upstairs to rooms brimming with art supplies and games. A computer room had computers on big and little tables for children of all ages. "There were no computers back in AJ's time," Ella said.

"But I just know he would have loved them."

They found Levi setting up a room. "What do you think of my Carpenter's Corner?" he asked. He was filling a pegboard with hammers and screwdrivers and pliers and chisels and sandpaper and boxes of nails and screws. Barrels overflowing with wood scraps stood all around.

Henry whistled. "I'd sure like to build something here."

Levi laughed. "I could use an assistant teacher on weekends," he said, "if you're interested."

"Yes," said Henry, grinning, "yes, I am."

"Now," Ella said, "Levi and I have a surprise for you."

The children followed them up to the attic. "AJ wanted children climbing up his rope ladder," said Ella. "He wanted them looking out the tower window. He wanted them to see the beauty of Greenfield the way he had seen it from the top of his reading rock. But not all children can climb as well as the four of you. So..."

"So..." Levi said as they reached the tower, "I built a little something."

The Fight for the Manor

The children stared. The tower was filled with ropes of all sizes and colors. Ropes knotted into ladders and tunnels and tubes. Rope bridges to walk across and rope nets to catch you if you fell. A thick bouncy pad covered the floor. The Aldens had a grand time climbing around Levi's invention. At last, they reached the secret reading room. They found colorful beanbag chairs where children could take books from the shelves and sit and read.

And that's just what the children did.

***

It seemed everyone in Greenfield came to the grand opening of AJ's Place. Inside, Ella and Levi led tours. In the backyard, Gus and his wife from Gus's Gas grilled hot dogs and hamburgers and corn on the cob. Anabel set up a Daisy's Dairy ice cream stand. Children slid down AJ's zigzag slides. They swung on wiggly swings. They climbed through fabulous forts. They squealed as they ran through shaky sprinklers. They dug for plastic dinosaur bones in a huge sandbox. They planted plants in the garden.

The Fight for the Manor

Henry, Jessie, Violet, and Benny tried everything. Finally, they joined Grandfather at a picnic table. As Benny rested, he looked up at the manor. Sunlight shone through the leaves of tall trees. It made shadows dance on the manor. Way up high, in Rapunzel's window, Benny saw a large shadow. Benny thought it looked like a man with a huge mustache. The man seemed to be waving his hand and smiling. Benny smiled and waved back. But when Benny blinked, the man was gone.

Turn the page to read a
sneak preview of

THE SEA TURTLE
MYSTERY

the next
Boxcar Children mystery!

Six-year-old Benny Alden was confused. He tilted his head to the side and looked at the map in his sister Violet's hands. Violet was ten, and she was helping teach Benny how to read the map. The two were in the back seat of Grandfather's car on their way to a place called Padre Island. Benny pointed. "I know this word says *island*, but I thought islands were round. This one looks like a big line on the map."

"Padre Island is a barrier island," said Henry from the front seat. Henry was the oldest of the Alden children. At fourteen, he had learned about different land formations in school. "Most barrier islands are long and narrow and not very far from land. They're kind of like big sandbars."

Benny's twelve-year-old sister Jessie spoke up next. "Look out the window! We're about to cross the bridge to the island!"

Within just a few minutes Grandfather pulled into a parking lot and stopped the car. It had been a long journey. But the view was worth it.

Behind them, seagrasses and flowering vines covered the sand dunes. The beach and the ocean were right in front of them. The four children jumped out and ran down to the water. Grandfather followed with Watch, the Aldens' wirehaired terrier.

Violet couldn't believe what she saw. "There are millions and millions of shells here!" she said, picking up a couple. "All different kinds too." She was so excited about the shells she didn't even notice when a big blue heron flew overhead.

"It's such a wide-open space. We can see for miles," said Jessie. "I'm going to take lots of pictures."

"Where are all the buildings?" asked Benny.

"There aren't any houses or shops on this part of the island," said Grandfather. "This is a National Seashore, which is a lot like a National Park. The land has been set aside so it can be protected."

Henry walked back toward the car to a sandy area in front of the dunes. "Jessie, don't you think this is a good place for the tent?" he asked. "It's close to the visitor center and the ranger station."

"Yes, it's perfect," said Jessie.

The children piled everything at the spot Henry had chosen. When they were finished and Grandfather was closing up the back of the car, a truck sped past them. It drove right off the road and onto the sand. Then it sped down the beach.

"I didn't know people could drive on the beach," said Henry. "That looks like fun."

"This seashore is very long," said Grandfather. "It would take a lot of time to travel all the way down it on foot. Vehicles help people to get there faster. There are speed limits, but you'll have to watch out for cars on the beach."

"We will," said Jessie.

"Are you sure you don't want to camp with us, Grandfather?" Benny asked.

Grandfather smiled. "I'm sure. I'll be happy sitting in a rocking chair on the porch of the inn back on the mainland. But when I see you in the evenings, you'll have to tell me all about your adventures."

The children promised they would, then said good-bye. After Grandfather had gone, the Aldens got to work setting up the tent and organizing the supplies. When they were done, Jessie looked over everything. She liked to keep things organized. "It looks like we have everything we need," she said.

"It's a lot more than we had when we lived in the boxcar," said Henry.

"That seems like such a long time ago," Violet said. "I can't believe we didn't even want to meet Grandfather back then."

After the Aldens' parents had died, the children had run away. They hadn't wanted to live with their grandfather because they were afraid he would be mean. They found an old boxcar in the woods and had lived in it until their grandfather found them. He turned out not to be mean at all! Now they lived with Grandfather back in Greenfield, Connecticut, and the boxcar was their clubhouse.

Jessie picked up her camera and put the strap around her neck. "It was nice of Grandfather to arrange this vacation for us. I don't know about everyone else, but I'm ready to explore the beach."

"Yay!" Benny yelled, running down to the ocean.

"The water is so warm!" he called to the others. He jumped up and down, splashing. Then all of a sudden he stopped and looked down. Then he looked back up at the others. Jessie could see that he was scared as he ran back to the beach.

"There's something in there!" he yelled. "It's after me!"

"Whoa, Benny, don't be scared," Henry said. "The water is too shallow for a big fish."

Jessie waded in and looked down at the water. "Sometimes the way the waves move over the sand makes it look like something is moving in the water. It's just a trick on your eyes."

"But I did see something," Benny said. He stretched his arms out as wide as he could. "Something this big."

Henry and Watch came to the edge of the water as a big wave came in and then rolled back. Watch barked and stepped back a few steps.

"There!" yelled Benny.

Where Benny pointed, a big clump of sand seemed to rise up from the sandy bottom. Watch barked again at the strange shape. Then another wave washed some of the sand away, revealing a strange-looking creature. Benny was right. There was something in the shallows. Something big!

Introducing The Boxcar Children Early Readers!

Adapted from the beloved chapter books, these new early readers allow kids to begin reading with the stories that started it all. Look for *The Yellow House Mystery* and *Mystery Ranch*, coming Spring 2019!

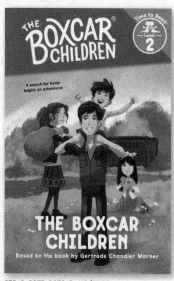

978-0-8075-0839-8 · US $12.99

978-0-8075-7675-5 · US $12.99

GERTRUDE CHANDLER WARNER discovered when she was teaching that many readers who like an exciting story could find no books that were both easy and fun to read. She decided to try to meet this need, and her first book, *The Boxcar Children*, quickly proved she had succeeded.

Miss Warner drew on her own experiences to write the mystery. As a child she spent hours watching trains go by on the tracks opposite her family home. She often dreamed about what it would be like to set up housekeeping in a caboose or freight car—the situation the Alden children find themselves in.

While the mystery element is central to each of Miss Warner's books, she never thought of them as strictly juvenile mysteries. She liked to stress the Aldens' independence and resourcefulness and their solid New England devotion to using up and making do. The Aldens go about most of their adventures with as little adult supervision as possible—something else that delights young readers.

Miss Warner lived in Putnam, Connecticut, until her death in 1979. During her lifetime, she received hundreds of letters from girls and boys telling her how much they liked her books.

978-0-8075-2850-1 · US $6.99

Introducing Interactive Mysteries!

Have you ever wanted to help the Aldens crack a case? Now you can with this interactive, choose-your-path-style mystery!

The Boxcar Children, Fully Illustrated!

This fully illustrated edition celebrates Gertrude Chandler Warner's timeless story. Featuring all-new full-color artwork as well as an afterword about the author, the history of the book, and the Boxcar Children legacy, this volume will be treasured by first-time readers and longtime fans alike.

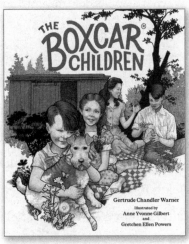

978-0-8075-0925-8 · US $34.99